DEATH MY
OWN WAY

Michael S. A. Graziano

DEATH MY OWN WAY

Leapfrog Press
Fredonia, New York

Published in 2012 in the United States by
Leapfrog Press LLC
PO Box 505
Fredonia, NY 14063
www.leapfrogpress.com

Printed in the United States of America

Distributed in the United States by
Consortium Book Sales and Distribution
St. Paul, Minnesota 55114
www.cbsd.com

First Edition

ISBN: 978-1-935248-33-0

Library of Congress Cataloging-in-Publication Data

TK

For D.

When you realize how perfect everything is you will tilt your head back and laugh at the sky.
—Siddhartha Gautama (c. 500 BC)

Life is suffering.
—Siddhartha Gautama

1

My clothes are now satisfactorily hanged at the top of the magnolia tree.

I'm six feet of hairy emaciation standing in the dirt at the foot of the tree. Curls of drizzle-damp hair straggle on my head, my face, my neck, my chest, grading into the curls on my stomach, my pubic mop, my legs, as if I'm wearing an old suit of mangy black funeral clothes with a hole cut in it to let my genitalia dangle through. My pelvic bones look like a juggling act, a carnivalesque triplet of lumps, one lump on the left balanced by two on the right. The extra lump, the upper right, is cancer.

I can smell body-sickness steaming in the cold air.

My feet pick up a layer of freezing mud as I walk away, flap flap, on what feels increasingly like hard rubber flippers instead of skin and flesh. I'm relishing the uniqueness of the sensation—chilled muddy pebbles in the cracks between my almost-numbed toes.

I find myself smiling benevolently, nodding absolution at the shocked expressions that I pass. I am sorry that so few skeptics are in the park at this time of night to behold my art. Not too many people stay out in a drizzle.

Maybe I can take up a permanent residence. The Naked Park Walker. A New York installation for months, for years. I won't need a job. I can ask the hotdog vendors for handouts and they would be happy to oblige me because of my advertisement value. If somebody asks, "Hey, Naked Park Weird Pelvis Man, where did you get that delicious looking chilly dog?" I can point back up the path and say, "Right there, Normal Everyday Man, see that yellow umbrella?"

I reach the end of the footpath. My way is blocked by a parapet, a waist high concrete railing, dark from the rain, grainy and pebbled, stuck with dead moss in patches. When I look over the wall I see a drop of about twenty feet to the street below. People must like to stand here during the day talking sporting events and office politics, drinking coffee as they gaze over the cityscape. An old cardboard cup sits on the wall filled with rainwater and a dead spider.

While I am leaning forward, the wall's pitted texture sharp against my elbows, I am aware of two or three people behind me staring at my hairy backside. The feel of their eyes on me is like a thumb massage. They've stopped at a distance and I hear them muttering to each other in a tone of confusion more than hostility. I don't turn around to face them. They don't bother me. Let them admire the pelt on my back.

What would happen if I climbed onto the wall and reared up on my hind legs, beating my chest pads, revealed to the world, to the highway below, lit by the cinematic wheeling, rushing headlights of cars and SUVs?

I am Gorilla! Hear me roar!

My primal spirit may be strong but my arms are not. I have trouble clambering onto my plinth. The sack of my gut, shriveled up from bad appetite, bangs against the concrete. I brace my palms on the wall and lean forward, kicking behind me, trying to wriggle onto my stomach while a pebble gets stuck in my navel and the people behind me mutter and the realization dawns on me that leaping up and roaring like a gorilla is beyond my capability.

Something is scratching my shoulder. I think it must be a branch poking me from the nearby tree but it turns out to be the fingernails of a hand. I turn and find a woman standing beside me, one hand plucking white earbuds out of her ears and the other hand on my shoulder yanking me away from the wall.

"What are you *doing*? Don't do that. You shouldn't do that."

Her voice is filled with urgency as if she has raccoons fighting each other in her throat.

I can't figure out the reason for the woman's anxiety. The interference seems presumptuous. Nobody owns this wall. It's public property. I can stand on it naked and roar if I want to.

Then I realize—she must think I'm trying to kill myself.

"It's a long way down," I admit, because I can't think of anything else to say.

"I know," she says. "You can't *do* that. It isn't worth it. You shouldn't do that. You need help, Mister. You need counseling, is what you need, not jumping off the. . . ."

She waves her hand, not entirely sure what to call the ledge.

I doubt the fall would kill me. But the traffic would, once I rolled into the highway.

She lets go of my shoulder and steps back. We

face each other in a pool of lamplight fragment-
ed through the winter-bare branches of a tree.

This is what I see.

I see a young woman with an urgent expression on her face, her hands raised, her fists
clenched as if she were about to box me. Her
hair is pulled back from her face in a ponytail.
A few loose strands are stuck to her forehead
in the drizzle. Her nose and her chin are both
sharp like teaspoons. She is wearing a gray baggy
sweat suit that hides the contours of her body,
but the thinness of her face and the energy of
her stance suggest that she is wiry underneath.
Her white sneakers are browning in a mud puddle.

She is an attractive magazine advertisement
and I am a naked grotesque bit of hairy gristle.
She should be terrified of a pervert in the park
at night. She should run in a panic. But she
is utterly unafraid of me. Her fear is all about
whether I'll jump. She doesn't seem to have any
concern for her own safety.

The woman is brassy enough to save a fellow
human being and I am the human being. The
logic of that relationship astonishes.

Who thought her up? Is she *prima facie* here,
neither created nor imagined, but of her own reality? Is she unique or is the city populated with

versions of her? Is she a New York phenomenon or do other cities have duplicates of the model?

Her behavior suggests a deep kinship to me. To confront me, to pull up sharp in the middle of her jogging, to interrupt her music and haul at a shoulder, is itself a metaphor. It is a gorgeous gesture of nonconformity. She is as much a creator of meaning as I am.

The world, I see in a moment of startled revelation, contains two people. The rest are automata. In my action tonight I've asked a question, more like bellowed it, shouted out a challenge, thumbed my ass hole at the world, and in her reaction she has answered the challenge with a magnificence that saves the honor of the universe.

2

A posse of heroes crashes into my moment of revelation.

"He's, um, attacking her!" one of them shouts. "And he tried to . . . to . . . to push her down on the ground! Or something! Did you *see* that?"

To be absolutely clear, I did *not* push her. She grabbed me. She clutched at my shoulder. I suppose shadows in the moonlight and the rain can play tricks especially on automata.

Three heroes join the moment, three men, one of them older in a tatty corduroy jacket that smells of cigarettes, two of them younger, gym-pumped, in matching green and black camouflage jogging sweats. They lunge forward. A hand clamps my wrist, an elbow crooks my neck from behind, my legs kick out reflexively as I lose my footing, something slips in the rain-slippery confusion, something bumps against something else, flesh against concrete, and the woman doubles over the railing. Wham! Wheee! She is gone, ipod and all.

I am hit in the stomach so hard that I black out. The world clenches around me, around the pain of being punched on a cancerous lump, and then slowly relaxes and expands again into normal space and time. I find I am on all fours in front of the wall vomiting into a puddle of mud water.

In the excitement of catching the perpetrator, the three heroes, much impressed with themselves, seem to have temporarily forgotten about the victim they had intended to rescue. They are standing over me, their fists balled, ready to knock me down again if I should try to run. I don't bother. I remain on my hands and knees, breathing hard, a strand of saliva connecting my lip to the water on the ground.

Truth, I muse, is expensive.

But what is the truth that I just bought? I can't remember. I had it clearly in mind just before I was attacked. Now my stomach hurts too much for me to concentrate. I know I did something terrible. That, at least, is what the world will think.

I'm not even sure how bad the terrible thing is. Probably worse than I am capable of imagining at the moment.

The drizzle hisses on the wet ground, the three heroes breathe loudly, one of them presses buttons on his cell phone with a shaky finger, the traffic grates and clatters, but behind this trivia of noise is a silence that sounds like a church bell. Bad news, it says. Good news, it says. You are lost. Humanity is saved.

3

Now five people are lined up along the concrete parapet. They are puppets looking over the gaudy board of a puppet theatre and I have a privileged backstage perspective. Their heads and upper bodies, topping the wall, jiggle in excitement. Two of the puppets are policemen in police hats and three are citizen heroes, previously introduced.

The policemen are shining flashlights over the wall. All five heads crane to see what happened to the woman who saved the honor of the universe.

Narratives spool out of this moment in all directions. She's been murdered by a pervert. She isn't dead yet. She's okay. She's mutilated. Her legs are broken. Her neck is broken. Her brain is squished out on the road like pizza dough. She can walk but her pants have a hole in the knee. She's laughing. She's gasping. She ran away. She was never here in the first place and we all imagined her. A trick of the light, you know.

In my own narrative the woman has set me free. She has confirmed me. She has *caused* me. She has given me hope.

But also, in an entirely pragmatic way that I appreciate just as much as the esoterica, the woman has freed me by distracting the authorities. They are so busy looking over the wall that they have forgotten about me.

I stand up and gingerly touch my stomach. I can still feel the pressure of a ghost fist, a little off center, just below the navel. I wipe my palms on my thighs to get the mud off my hands, wipe a dangling strand of mucus from the corner of my mouth onto the back of my wrist, grimace, take a deep breath, and walk away. As simply as that. I walk away. I am not sneaking. I am not trying to escape. I am simply walking, more like limping, the slap and suck of my feet on the wet ground perfectly clear, at least to me, and nobody turns to look. I won't bother with them if they don't bother with me.

I feel light-headed.

My emotion is overwhelming.

A combination of blunt trauma, standing, and stretching has helped to dislodge the emotion from somewhere in my gut and now peristalsis brings it up the rest of the way. The surge of feeling is like an uncontrollable bout of vomiting. I don't even know how to categorize the experience. It is terror. It is elation. It is wonder, and anxiety, and joy, and sadness, and it is freedom, and it is pure experiential vividness. It is the realization that I am actually here in the state that I am actually in. It is the potency of reality. It is a tremble that runs up and down my body. The tremble might be from the cold, though.

I am guilty of murder.

Happenstance killed her. Bad luck killed her. Overzealous Samaritans killed her. I know. But I was the ultimate cause. I can't escape the facts: I am. She was. To deny that I killed her would be an act of disrespect, and I can't disrespect someone who helped to create me as I am at this moment in time.

4

Watch me run full tilt down the grade of a path, a black macadam path winding through the deserted park, my arms out to either side crucifixion style, my hands open, my fingers splayed, my feet slapping loudly on the ground in a lopsided cancer-induced limp, the wrinkled sack of my gut bouncing, my head tilted back, my eyes winking and cringing in the drizzle, the water falling into my open mouth and tapping on the back of my throat.

"She's dead! Ha ha! She's dead! She's deaaaaaad!"

Now here is a man walking toward me. He is wearing a long tan raincoat that blends into the mud and the bare brown trees or I would have seen him at a distance. He emerges out of the shadows directly in front of me with his face and hands glowing. He could be an angel in human form, his spiritual light imperfectly cloaked by the raincoat, his purpose—to save me? To inspire me? To condemn me? To give me absolution? To arrest me? I am actually afraid of him.

But I see it now. He's texting. The blue-green light comes from a mobile device that he's cradling in his hands.

I stop, frozen in mid melodramatic flail of head, tongue, arms, and fingers, while his gaze rakes over my body.

"Just so you know," he says, "that's really annoying. That shouting."

"I killed my mother."

"Yes, that's nice. She took one look at you and croaked. I'm trying to text here. Is that all right? I mean, do I have permission? Can I pay attention to what I'm typing, instead of to the Central Park lunatic brigade?"

The angel walks away muttering, "Get a life, Idiot."

His sphere of otherworldly glow disappears in the haze and I am alone again, in silence, frozen in mid crazy-flail contortion.

My shouting frenzy is over.

My arms flop down and my tongue crawls back into my mouth.

I don't mind the opinions of a curmudgeonly angel—my emotions right now are too large for such minor considerations as embarrassment or resentment—but the encounter has helped me to see the uselessness of shouting. My emotions are inexpressible. They are misfitting shapes inside me. They are killing me. They are worse than the cancer. As much as I feel like running through the night screaming, it is really too prosaic a way to express the enormity of the moment. Lacking any useful option I keep the emotions uneasily to myself and walk quietly in the rain deeper into the park.

5

The park is empty now. No movement or sound other than the jitter of the trees in the wind. A few soggy newspapers caught trembling around the legs of benches. A few trashcans so overstuffed that a cup or a balled up wrapper occasionally drops off the top of the pile and hits the ground with a soft plop. The pattering of the rain and the slapping of my feet on the pavement. I can barely see the pavement—only just well enough to follow it. The light is a nocturnal city glow reflected from the clouds, a dim dirty smear of gray. Occasionally I pass a streetlamp and the drizzle suddenly becomes visible, piercing the cone of light.

My legs begin to ache. I am hardly in physical condition to walk far. When I notice an involuntary tremble in my right foot, when my breath catches on phlegm and the tendons at the back of my neck hurt so much from holding up the weight of my head that they feel like they are about to tear, then I give up my journey, slouch across the wet grass, and sit on a bench by the side of the lake.

All paths lead to the lake.

I sit on the edge of the bench, hunched, shivering, head tucked down, shoulders peaked, arms around my skinny chest, hands clutching my elbows, feet curled and trembling against the ground. I am defeated. I've lost. I don't even know what game I was trying to win.

I've always imagined the park at night to be a dangerous place owned by roving gangs and rabid raccoons. But I am alone. I am sitting in silence and in darkness. The air is not quite cold enough to freeze the surface of the lake, and the drizzle, falling on that large sheet of water, makes a quiet, immense background sound like an interminable exhalation.

The nighttime secrets of the park unfold.

An opossum crawls through the mud at the edge of the lake and stares at me beadily. Lampposts reflect in his black pebble eyes. I nod to him, to which he bares his insectivorous teeth and continues on his way.

I hear a thump on the ground behind me. It

sounds like the hoof of a deer stepping out shyly
for the evening to nibble on the grass. When I
turn to look over my shoulder I give a phlegmy
squeak, a start, and suppress the reaction in an
instant. The thump was no deer. A person is
standing just behind the bench looking at me.
He's a little man, skinny in ragged jeans and a
flannel jacket. Pale bits of beard and mustache
and mangy fur stick out of his head all directions. He looks like the spirit of Central Park—
of the leafless, littered Central Park at midnight
in winter.

6

His small square of a mouth is open in innocence.

"Did you really kill your mother?" he asks anxiously. "Is that really true?"

I stare at him.

"I can't believe that's really true. You wouldn't be running around shouting about it. Which by the way is . . . *anarchic*," he says with some admiration mixed in with the anxiety.

"Have a seat," I suggest.

He sits shyly next to me. The stanchions of the bench are concrete and the seat is made of plastic planks molded and grained and colored to look like wood. Since the plastic boards are pooled with water, the seat of his pants must be soaked. He doesn't seem to care.

"What's your name?" I ask. For all my anarchy, you see how I stick to the formalities. I don't know what else to say to him.

"Bottle Rat. Well," he adds, giving me a sidelong glance, as if a little frightened at his own boldness, "that's not my real name. But my specialty is bottle caps. So I'm Bottle Rat."

I've never heard of that particular specialty before. My face must show something of my question.

"Do you want to see a bottle cap?" he offers. "I've been working on it all day."

He digs his boney fingers into the front pocket of his jeans and brings out the bottle cap, if that is what it is. He hunches over it, peering intently in the dim light, straightening this and that part of it with pinched nail-tips, and then sits back and holds it out for me to see.

A tiny red bird sits on his open palm. It is perfect. Its feathers are individually teased. Its head is at a slight tilt as if the bird were listening to the pulse in the little man's hand and thinking about worms. It has so much life and yet so much delicacy, and is so absurdly small, about the size of a locust, that I feel tenderness toward it and want to cup it in my hands and protect it. Judging by its color, it must once have been a coke cap.

I stare at Mr. Rat in amazement.

"I, um, chew them," he says with a shrug as pride struggles visibly through the shyness in his disorganized little face. "I work the plastic with my teeth. Didn't you ever chew a plastic bottle cap? Or a straw? I used to do straws. But the possibilities were, you know, limited. I've been on bottle caps for almost a year now."

The casual way he stuffs the bird back into his pants pocket disturbs me as if he were disrespecting a living thing.

"I do one or two a day," he says. "That's how I make my living. I'm riff-raff, you know. I'm a park loony. I thought maybe you were too, that's why I came over. I can spot them," he says with great earnestness. "There you are naked and screaming about killing your mother and there's no smell of alcohol." He takes a sniff to confirm. "So you must be a lunatic too. A non-conformist, is how I think of it. An artist, you know. A rebel. A subversive. An individualist. An anarchist. A maverick. A talent. A free-thinker. Dregs of society and proud of it. Counter-culture, like one of us." He strikes his chest with the tips of all five fingers as if trying to break through his rib cage and get a grasp on his heart.

Even though he talks too much, he has such an innocent and serious manner that I already like him. I am grateful for his company. The distraction eases my mind. I loosen my grip on my elbows, lean back until my spine rests against the wet plastic boards, and relax as much as I can while shivering.

7

"How many of you anarchists are in the park?" I
ask.

"Oh, lots. A whole Central Park Society. If you're
a non-conformist, you should join us. We thought
about calling it the Antisocial Society. But one of
us used to be a shrink, and she said that antisocial
means you go around and kill people, and none
of us does that anymore. You should think about
visiting us. Unless you have somewhere else to
go back to. Did you really kill your mother?"

I think for a moment because I want to answer
honestly. Then I tell him, "Yes and no."

He sits quietly waiting for my explanation and
I find his patience, after the prattle, lovely and
encouraging.

"I met her for the first time tonight," I admit. The first time you meet your mother is when you are born. Therefore I must have been born tonight and my mother must have died in childbirth. Which makes a great deal of sense to me. I shrug and spread out my hands palm-up, by which I really mean that I wish I had a beautiful little red bird on each of my palms. Maybe they would lift me out of my reality. "I don't know if she's dead. If she is, I didn't push her. Somebody else did. But I was nearby and somehow a part of it all. I don't feel good about it."

"I love metaphors," Bottle says softly, and I am certain that he understands me. I feel a warmth for him.

"She fell over a wall," I add.

"So did I, so did I," Bottle says. "So did a lot of us. Sometimes the world is better on the other side of the wall."

Our literals and metaphors have gotten mixed up but I don't bother to correct him.

"Do you live in the park?" I ask.

"In the boathouse," he says. "There's a way you can get in at the back."

"Is it a nice place?"

"Are you house hunting?" He gives me a sudden smile, his little square mouth opening up and showing me a grille of skinny, long, browning teeth. I feel sorry for him. He looks as delicate as his plastic bird and just as much like a piece of recycled garbage. "There's some prime real estate nearby. Vacancies under the gazebo floor."

"I might look into it," I say.

He hesitates politely and then asks, "Why did you go naked?"

I shrug. I am not sure how to put it. "I couldn't stand the polyester on me anymore."

"Oh!" He nods vigorously. "That's understandable! Me, I always get a rash from polyester. And rayon. I don't like rayon."

"No, I mean something else. My life was polyester melted onto me and I had to get it off. It was disgusting and I had to get it off. It turned out to mean so little. Not that it was a bad life, but it was just a covering . . . I don't know how else to say it. I don't even know who I am anymore. It's hard to tell your covering from who you are. Well, I'm going existential on you."

Bottle sighs with pleasure. "You sound like a book. The rest of the club will love you. A naked philosopher meditating in the park at midnight?"

He jumps up wiry and enthusiastic, shedding droplets of water, shaking his tufted hair, clapping his wet hands, and says, "You have *got* to come. We're having a meeting tonight. We meet whenever it rains, because everybody gets in under the same shelter. You're my guest. At least come in and find out what we're about! Will you?"

He does a little rat dance in front of me and I can't refuse that ridiculous dance of excitement.

8

An ache is spreading slowly from the punch site in my gut through the rest of my body, filling up the space where all my normal sensation has been dulled by the cold. I'm unsteady when I stand up. I am shaky in the legs, but I can still follow Bottle's wiry step.

He leads me up a muddy footpath sharply away from the lake, then squeezes through a slot between two concrete restrooms, crunches over gravel, scrambles up an embankment, across a soggy lawn, and brings me to a gazebo. Maybe it's the one with vacancies under the floor. It's large, could fit a crowded thirty people under that conical wooden roof, though it looks empty from the outside. A lamppost about fifty feet away provides the only light.

As we approach I can smell the wood. It isn't painted. It's roughed, bare, natural wood, dark from the rain. The wet must bring out the musky smell of lumber. The structure is pentagonal. It has a wooden balustrade around all sides with a gap for the stairs. The rainwater, streaming off the roof, has carved a moat a few inches deep, needles of water falling into mud, the muddy water spreading away from the gazebo and losing itself eventually in the grass. My feet sink into the mud.

The stairs are three steps, bare splintery wood, and Bottle Rat jumps up, hops up all three steps at a time, leaps through the beaded curtain of water falling from the eves, and lands like an acrobat half crouched. I step up carefully to avoid splinters in the soles of my feet, although I doubt I would feel any in my foot-chilled state. I stand lopsided and trembling behind Bottle Rat's skinny dancer's crouch.

"Everyone!" he announces grinning with an impresario's gesture toward me, "Gentlemen! Ladies! LGBT! Christians! Heathens! Humanists! Nobodies! I bring you. . . ."

He pauses dramatically, hops and lands again, crouching, facing a different direction and another segment of his audience.

Then hops and lands a third time, facing a third way.

"I bring you Found Art! Am I not good? Am I not just so, so good?"

9

I feel a collision of emotions. Pride. It is an honor to be treated as an aesthetic inspiration. Outrage. It is ignominious and a little unnerving to be led to the center of an altar and displayed. I've been reified. I've been deceived. I've been glorified. I've been de-humanized.

I keep my peace and stand without a word, shivering, looking at my audience, dripping onto the wood planking. The rain is no longer on me and a warmish human exhalation surrounds my body like ectoplasm. The warmth is both delicious and painful.

The audience is not extensive. Four ragged people are sitting on the floor and leaning back against the railing. Five including Bottle Rat. I wonder if I am expected to sit on the floor with them or stand where I am.

"Give him a chair," somebody says.

The one calling for a chair has a guitar in his lap and the guitar says Yogurt in red paint on the wood, enigmatic and barely legible in the dimness. The man is old and skinny with bushy white hair, his face deeply lined, his back hunched under flannel, and he reminds me of Geppetto.

"Give him a chair," he says and plucks a string. The E string. Plonk.

"Got it," someone else says, crawling to her feet. "I do love a nice hairy naked man. Let's get him settled in a better perspective."

She puts her hands on the wooden balustrade that encircles the gazebo. For a moment I see her clearly against the rain, the lamppost behind her. She is skinny, young, straggle-haired, happy, not so young on closer look, wiry, a competence in her fingers and a confidence in her face and a commotion in the rattling glass beads looped and looped around her neck. She vaults over the railing and disappears with a splash.

Another member of the audience is sitting in plaid shorts with his knees peaked, his arms wrapped around his shins, his face tucked down as he chews idly on some leg hairs sticking out of his left kneecap, his large dark eyes looking up at me in open curiosity.

The final member of the audience is all cloak.

Something angular sticks up over the railing. "Take it," the woman's voice says. "Quickly. It's slippery."

Plaid Shorts Knee Hair Chewer stands and takes the chair. It is a wet, old, loose, metallic office chair with chipped black paint and rusty wheels.

The woman clambers over the railing and wipes water from her lean face. Her clothes are soaked. Her beads are drooling water. The evening may have started with a light drizzle but the rain is falling hard now, pounding on the wooden roof above us so that I have trouble hearing voices.

The chair is placed at the center of the pentagonal floor and I am guided and seated, evidently a statue arranged to advantage on a pedestal. I'm grateful for the seat anyway.

I've lost feeling in my flesh. When I shift my weight in the chair I expect my buttock meat to shatter into frozen bits, and am surprised instead to be sitting on a thin gluteus pillow that moves with the consistency of chicken grease. My ribs hurt from the cold. That is a good sign. They are not frozen yet. My back, my spine, my neck, my shoulders, I don't mind the cold on them, as if the freezing sensation were a shell hardening on me. My testicles wobble at the edge of the chair. My penis is so shriveled from the cold that it looks more like a wound than a worm. A few heavy drops of water make their way through the shingles on the roof and land on my scalp at unpredictable times, as if someone were tapping me hard with the tip of a finger to remind me of something. I can't remember what.

In silence the five people contemplate me. An eagerness in momentary check. An appreciation. A communal pause of anticipation. Five grotesques, unpredictables, sprites, shadows, variously-costumed grim reapers, midnight revelers, drifters, members of a celestial tribunal convened to judge me?

I accidentally breathe in a droplet of rainwater that was dangling on my upper lip. I choke on it, gasp, hack, sputter, turn my head, and spit it back out on the floor.

The act breaks the silence.

The five people begin to talk.

10

"We need a placard for the piece. What's the title on the placard?" says the beaded lady who fetched the chair. Chair Lady is sitting on the floor, leaning back against the damp wooden posts of the railing. Her legs are stretched in front of her. Her arms are crossed over her chest, covered by the cascade of her beaded necklaces. The posture makes her look as if she has tucked her hands under her shirt, a gesture comfortable, casual, and self satisfied.

"Idiot commits suicide by self exposure," says the cloaked person, in a muffled voice. I think Cloak is a man with a feminine voice. Or a woman with a smoky voice. The hooded head turns and gapes black toward me, exhaling darkness.

Guitar says, "Plonk," then, "Ping,"—his guitar is beautifully in tune!—for an old man so damp and miscellaneous I expected a jangle, not a professional sonority—and he says, meditatively, quietly, and I can barely hear him over the drumming of the rain, and Cloak turns its yawning face toward him, and everyone else turns an ear, "Nakedness is such a powerful hue." He pauses, then lifts his hand from the guitar, spreads his fingers wide, palm outward, makes a sweeping sideways gesture to block out the imaginary placard: "VULNERABILITY."

A collective "Ah!" of satisfaction.

This frayed old man has the right to talk about vulnerability. They are all as vulnerable as I am. I am simply a literal depiction of the communal truth.

"Nothing from you," says Cloak in a soft, menacing, grim-reaper-ish voice while a swift lump, evidently a fisted hand with a finger pointed under the cloak, bounces in my direction. "We don't want your back story. We don't need it, thank you."

"Oh, honestly," sighs Chair Lady. "You don't need to be rude. The man is cold and starved half to death. Look at him. He's so . . . you know . . . *vulnerable.*"

"I don't want my artistic opinion to be contaminated by his narrative," Cloak insists.

"Keep him under control," Knee agrees. "Otherwise you never know what these crazy riff-raff people might put over on us. As soon as we let him talk he'll start asking for money. You'll see. Or food," he says, bending his head down to chew on his knee hair again. "Not that we have any," he adds mumbling. He spits pieces of hair onto the floor. I can see them flying out of his mouth, sparkling for an instant in the light from the distant lamppost. Hair and teeth. An aura of death about the man. About all five people.

Since I don't intend to ask for food or money, I begin to shake my head, but the finger-pointed lump in the cloak bounces back toward me as a warning and I stop in the middle of my gesture. I keep my mouth shut and my body still within the limits of my shivering. I don't mind. I find it comforting to sit still and let somebody else decide who I am.

"I had a fantastic chat with him," Bottle Rat says happily. He is sitting behind me. "I won't tell you what he said so I don't ruin anything."

"All right, it ruins it," Chair Lady admits. "Nothing worse than the artist's statement, a pile of misdirection getting in the way of the love affair between you and the art." The way she enunciates "love affair" almost has a meaning to me, rolling as though savored in her larynx. A fluid vocal gesture like so many of her other gestures. "But why can't the statement be a part of the art? A sculpture that talks. And asks for food. Or shelter. Or a raincoat. Or friendship. Or spare change. Change for coffee. A buck fifty for a hamburger. Well, all art talks, doesn't it? Maybe it's a part of the art when the sculpture ups and starts telling you about what ism it belongs to. Antidisestablishmentarianism. Ironic post modernism. Constructive deconstructivism. Weirdhip-ism. What's up with his middle region? What is he, some leftover iron slag?"

"Quasimodo," suggests Knee.

"He has a limp," Bottle Rat says. "I noticed that when he was following me here."

"Looks like he has more than a limp," Guitar says wisely. "An injury maybe."

All eyes examine my hips.

"All right, all right, that's enough," Chair Lady murmurs. Her eyes are half closed, maybe partly in laziness, maybe partly in annoyance. Despite her understated manner she seems to be the moderator of the group. "We're taking pot shots. I think we know how to be more systematic." She jingles an arm from under her beads and points with a languid gesture, her narrow wrist and hand elegantly relaxed, two fingers together as if she were too lazy to separate one finger, an unconscious beauty in her casual manner, gesturing in a circle that encompasses the audience. "Who wants to be first?"

11

A foot stretches out and kicks at my chair, sending me rotating to the right in a lopsided spin on loose squeaky bearings. When I come to rest the audience gains a new perspective on the art object. The lamppost light touches me from the side, glittering through droplets of water in my body hair.

"I'll start," says the druidic Cloak, a blue-jeaned leg and sneakered foot disappearing swiftly under the hem. The jeans and sneakers detract somewhat from the aura of druidic mystery.

The audience is silent.

The cloaked head bows as though in prayer.

"Anyway. Art isn't about the object. The object

is nothing. An act of misdirection. Art is about the audience.

"Look at the five of us. Look at how we've nudged ourselves into perfectly equal distances. A human trick. We pick the spaces around us. Something in us always strategizing. So we sit in a pentagon. Like a Wiccan ritual. Or a five pointed compass. The wind's five corners. The five elements. The five humors. The five horsemen. The five sides of a parallelogram. The five lobes of the brain. The five dimensions of spacetime. The five electrons of a beryllium atom. Makes you wonder what strange hyper-dimensional part of the human topography we span."

The hood bobs and turns, peering one way, the other, looking at the members of the pentagon as the dim light picks out a reddish thread or a silver thread here and there in the dark gray fabric of the cloak.

"Now look closely at the threads between— from Naked Man on his chair to me, from him to you, from him to each of us, radiating. He is radiant. He's radiating threads. Another thread from me to you, to you, to you. Oh go ahead, do the math. It's fifteen connecting threads. Each to each. All to all. It's a pentagonal spider web. It's macramé. It's the secret connectivity of life. It's art. When we look at him and talk about art, we're talking about that web, even if we don't all know it. We're not talking about him. We're talking about how we see him. How I see him. How I see that you see him. How I see that you see that I see him. But never how he sees me. We pretend that Art is the object sitting on the platform in front of us, the mimesis, the representation, but the object is only the peg at the center of the web. The peg has no soul of its own. It simply holds up the web. The measure of the peg is whether it's strong enough to support the macramé. Do you see? This is the essence of Art. Do you understand?"

A moment of silence follows Cloak's offering as if the thought is itself an art object to be appraised. I am not sure how I feel about having no soul of my own. I am, evidently, nothing more than a psychological nexus for the five people around me.

Guitar stirs and says, his head to the side, his mild voice blended partly into the rain, his hand spread over the strings as though hushing them so that he can hear his own thought better, "Very pretty. Very organized. Very science. But I smell some cruelty in it."

Chair Lady nods decisively. "I agree. What, to turn him into art is to take away his selfhood? It's nonsense."

"Art *is* cruel," Cloak says. "It can be, anyway. Don't blame me for the cruelty. It's inherent in the situation. Look at what we're doing to the man. Are you any less cruel? Propping him in front of us? We're replacing his soul with something much more complicated. Our own imaginations. How awful is that, taking us for the moment as a five-pointed sampling of the public? And public exposure isn't, after all, voyeurism, because we don't see people as they actually are. That would be kindness in comparison. No, we reconstruct them. We see them with a kind of vileness that creeps into the public opinion. Isn't that the whole point of Art: to replace the truth of the object with the opinions of the audience?"

Collective silence. Collective think.

"Nice speech," says Chair Lady, shaking beads of water from her beaky nose. An expression of skepticism bordering on dislike settles into the creases around her mouth. I sense that she has a long-running argument with Cloak. "I admire your cleverness. A⁺, Professor, but I'm just not feeling your definition of art."

Maybe the cruelty of the circumstance has heightened my instincts. My genitals stir subtly toward Chair Lady and I make no effort to hide the squishy motion. I believe she is to be my champion. She is defending my right to have a soul, anyway. I like her and I instinctively dislike Cloak.

"Take half a think at what you just said," she mutters, rolling her eyes. "Art is nothing more than a vile public profile? Really? Is that what you mean?"

Knee eagerly lifts his head and cuts in. "Oh, yes, good."

Knee's eagerness has a quality of self-advancement. I wonder if he is a failed corporate climber. He is trying to impress somebody with something. His face is thin, tight over his cheekbones, but sags around the jaw line as though he has lost weight recently. The skin under his chin jiggles when he moves his head, and because of the jiggle it's difficult for me to take his words seriously. He looks too needy. He looks too hungry.

"Oh I like that," he says fervently. "Oh now we're getting somewhere. Oh you mean an internet profile? You mean we turn ourselves into art? You mean that our naked weird hip guy, sitting on a chair, dripping cold, dying of exposure, with his equipment hanging off the edge flapping in our faces, so to speak, *bleeeah, gaahhhh*, showing us everything and saying nothing—this is The Modern Person with Online Profile,

Facebook Myspace Twitter Youtube Video kind of exhibitionistic reality TV fame addiction-to-texting carpal-tunnel self-cutting see-my-vlog thing? Public exposure of the grotesque kind? This is what we modern humans do to ourselves? This is what the sculpture stands for?" He shouts in nervous laughter then raises his hand and with a sideways gesture, imitating Guitar but with less authority and more of a nervous twitch, blocks out a new title for me, intoning: "Privacy in the Modern World." Then he lowers his hand and clutches his leg again, pulling his knee closer to his mouth.

His eyes flick to the side. Yes, he is posturing for Chair Lady. His spew of words and his clever social observations are for her. I watch her closely and see no reaction. He is too puny for her and his plaid shorts are too threadbare and his nervous tick of chewing his leg hair makes him look too much like a rabbit. Am I unkind? I think I am jealous. I am satisfied that she never glances toward him. She is looking at me thoughtfully.

"Certainly the world is exposure happy," she says. "I'd hardly deny that. And certainly this particular specimen is exposed. Bravo for noticing the connection. I'm just questioning whether public exposure, by itself, is the definition of art. More like martyrdom."

"He's martyred," Knee barks eagerly. "That's deep." If he wants to impress Chair Lady or flatter her, he is succeeding admirably in annoying her.

"Which makes him," says Guitar with a metallic *ping* like a nail, "Jesus."

"Now we're crucifying him!" Chair Lady shouts, shaking her head, droplets flying off her nose.

"But he *is* crucified," says Guitar in his soft voice. "Wasn't the heart of crucifixion the public exhibition?"

"We're gawkers around the cross," Knee explains.

"I know we are," Chair Lady mutters. "We're gawkers around each other's crosses and we're all crucified. I'm sure that's right—how could it not be?—but how ordinary is that insight? And how cynical? It's too cynical for me. I don't like the discussion. It starts right away with geometry, with the mathematics of a pentagon, and has no room for the human spirit. It lacks compassion. It's cold. It's calculus. It's cruel to the man."

"Really, I think he's okay," says Knee diplomatically. "I think he looks comfortable."

Chair Lady's head snaps up, she turns, she yells, "How can he look comfortable? Look at the poor man!"

Knee is abashed. His attempt to propitiate has failed. He's been slapped down. The loose skin under his chin wobbles. He ducks his head and nibbles furiously on his leg hair.

The tribunal is silent for a moment. The silence allows the conversation to relax from its spasm of anger. Chair Lady has traveled the distance from calm, languid, her eyes half closed, to an explosion of anger and a shout, a snarl with a bit of teeth, and I begin to wonder just how much the others are tweaking her on purpose to get a reaction. Guitar in particular seems to have a quiet way of manipulating her. His face, mainly in shadow, shows a hint of a smile.

"When I was little," Bottle Rat says into the silence, "I thought the word was comf-ter-ful."

The word passes around the circle as people try it in their mouths. Comf-ter-ful. Comf-ter-ful.

"That's like full of comf-ter," says Cloak.

"That was the idea," Bottle Rat admits. "My mom tried to correct me but I didn't believe her. For a long time I didn't like the sound if I said it the right way."

"We have here a martyr," muses Guitar, "spread out and crucified for our gawking pleasure, with a look of comf-ter on his face. Not comfort, but comf-ter. The not-quite-true version of the word that we can't get out of our minds and that we put on our faces to confront the public world."

"Then you've turned him into an indictment of us all," says Chair Lady, shrugging. "Congratulations on a cynical view of art."

Cloak lets out a low laugh partly muffled in fabric. "See how easy it is to get trapped when you think about Art as standing for something in particular? Then we end up arguing uselessly over the nature of that particular. He's a symbol of Jesus? He represents martyrdom? He represents an exposure-happy compulsively online modern world? He represents an ironic smile that itself represents us? He represents an entire theory of art—the theory of found art. Found wandering the park at night presumably looking for something of his own to find. He represents anti-art. He represents moral art—because he is a moral indictment of us. Does he really? Doesn't this obsession with representation miss the point? Do we need to collapse the wave function? Isn't he a thousand things and a thousand ways of acting on us, and the consequent ways that we act on each other and then react to each other? Isn't all art performance art—the performance of the audience? Action and reaction and re-reaction? Resonance instead of representation?"

"Aren't you asking a fricking lot of questions?" Knee says. He seems moody after Chair Lady's put down. "Oops. Pardon my existence. Here's what I think. I think you lectured on long enough and it's *my* turn now. That's what I think."

12

Nervous Flabby-Jowled Chewer of Knee Hair raises his left hand like a knife and begins to chop at the empty air. He chops to make his points. He begins by arranging the points in his mind, chopping for his own benefit, hacking at the air a few times before he speaks.

"Now I have to come up with something clever." He laughs at himself with a touch of shrillness, of performance anxiety I think, of resentment and self-resentment. "Look. We found a naked guy. And we're discussing him. And sure, I can see, we're discussing what I think of what you think of what I think you're thinking. I can see the threads going back and forth. I'm not blind. I can see the macramé. But I want to talk about the *man*. Not us. Not our interactive . . . hyperactive . . . pentographic connectivity. *Him*."

He frowns and chops at the shadows a few more times to organize his thoughts.

"You think he's sick. Somebody said he's Quasimodo. Oh, maybe I said that. Somebody said he's dying. I'm not denying that interpretation. I'm just saying, I don't think he came here to kick the bucket. I can't believe it. This stunt isn't some sicko suicide by exposure. Why did a man take off his clothes and run into the park? Why else? Because he's got *vitality*." That point receives an especially vigorous chop. "Think how much brashness it takes to do a thing like that. He came here to take a try at being *alive*." Chop. "It's perfectly obvious."

Another few chops.

"You said he was the picture of vulnerability. Yeah yeah. Maybe so. That's too easy. A naked body in a chair in the cold—Vulnerability. Nice. Boring. Obvious. But most of the time vulnerable people hide under something. Fashionable clothes. Routine. A *cloak*. An attitude. Right? Isn't that the definition of vulnerability? A strident asshole? Isn't it?" he says stridently, glaring around. "But here's a guy who doesn't feel the need to hide. He's right out here, right in front of us, just who he fucking is, and that means he's not anything like vulnerable. Or if he is, if naked is vulnerable, then it's also got a whopping big dose of ego mixed in. The guy is potent.

"Now, why are we here, the five of us? If you want to talk about us. If that's really part of the art, to talk about the audience. Why do we plop him down in the middle and go banging on and on about him? I mean, why does the man fascinate? And he does, too. We don't invite in any old bit of moldy sculpture. It's not because he's vulnerable. Nobody really likes to look at vulnerability. That makes people cringe. No, it's exactly because he's potent. We *admire* the guy. We're smelling the life in him and we want it for ourselves. We're like bats, man, we're drinking his blood.

"The scent of blood. I'm telling you.

"If it's okay for me to expand a little on the thought. I sold my last ratty old copy of Homer to a used bookstore for some acid. Well okay I didn't. That's a fantasy. But I just want to remind you of an old story. A traveler, ancient mariner, wise old salt dude, guy who's brave enough to let himself be vulnerable when he needs to be, takes a trip into the underworld. Nothing more underworld than Central Park at night. He's there because he's got a question for a ghost. You see, he's looking for knowledge." He taps his emaciated temple dramatically. "So he can find his way home. So he can find himself, know who he is, claim back his own. So he can be *alive*. Why else do you go to the land of the dead and back again? In search of your *life*, man.

"Well, it turns out it's hard to get the shades in hell to talk. They're shy, somehow. So this guy, he brings a bucket of blood with him. Ox blood, I think. The shades smell the blood. It's cocaine to them. They've been without life for so long that they *flow* toward it, shove each other out of the way to get at it and guzzle it. That's how they get seduced into talking. That's the story. And what I think I'm saying is," a nod to everyone around the circle, "that's who we are. We're the shades. We smell the vitality in the guy. We smell his honesty. We want the blood. We're yakking it up around the blood, just like the shades do in hell. That's art, man. Art is blood. Art is blood. Blood to a shade. Seems to me, your regular person, all of us, we're almost always emotional shades, mental shades, shades of gray, desperate for some vitality. Our whole ridiculous discussion of the theory of art is just shades talking, talking, talking because we drunk the blood of the art."

Suddenly I see myself alive, strong, dignified, earthy, virile, potent, courageous, seizing the moment, seizing the park, seizing the night, seizing myself, seizing my own identity, Olympian, Odyssean, resting in a circle of adulation. I sustain them.

How flattery does seduce.

"A much warmer view of the art object than our last bloodless theory," Chair Lady admits, and so Knee has scored a success, and glows, and grins, and reveals blond fragments of hair stuck between his teeth glittering in the partial light.

"Our souls are nothing but shadows on the gazebo wall," Guitar says with his ironic half smile. "How deliciously anti-Platonic."

"But what I really want to know," Chair Lady says thoughtfully, "is: who is Tiresias?"

A startled laugh rises up anonymously.

"If there are no volunteers," says Chair Lady, brow wrinkled, so much earnestness in her face that I know she's hiding a smile, "I nominate our elder statesman," jerking her head toward Guitar, wet locks of her blond hair flicking toward him and then laying flat against her cheek with a tiny slapping sound. I'm not sure I hear the sound. I may be imagining it. I hear a rattle of her glass beads.

"I'm Tiresias?" he says, looking up surprised.

"Who's Tiresias?" Bottle Rat asks timidly.

"The old white-haired sage," Knee explains.

"The ghost that the traveler dude wants to visit. Central Park at night homeless I mean *residence displaced* in winter, in the rain, good enough as the underworld. Okay and the flood on the grass out there, that's the river Styx." He points here and there with stubby fingers as if stage directing a play. "Our naked guy, he's the hero paying us a visit from the land of the living. We're shades sniffing around, and you," nodding to Guitar, "you're the celebrity ghost, you're the shade of the wise old man of the ancient world. You have the *knowledge*." Tapping his head again.

Guitar shrugs in a gesture of resignation and shakes his head. "No one quite so breezy as old Tiresias," he tells us, hunching and twisting his neck to get a better look at his fingers on the fingerboard, his old fluffy hair falling over one side of his face, the crease on the other side of his mouth drawn deep and strong in the light and shadow as he silently fingers a complicated piece. "He knew a little too much, Tiresias. Consequently the gods, in a fit of petulance, turned him into," here he pings a high vibrating note, "a woman."

Bottle Rat giggles. I can't see him—he's sitting behind me—but I can imagine his toothy rat look of grade-school hilarity.

"Pardon the stupidity of a nuclear physicist,"

Cloak says irritably. "But what's the sense in that? I like my science better, thank you. What is it with these useless old myths? Tell me: did he at least enjoy the experience?"

"Seems to have," Guitar says, shrugging. "He went and got married, anyway. I mean *she* got married. She had children too. But after a few years—"

"After a few years," Chair Lady interrupts, her left hand suddenly jerked out from under her beads, a knife chop of the hand through the air, vigorously with a rattle, evidently in mockery of Knee, whose gesture she has appropriated, a severe knife chop with a squeaky grunt as though decapitating the luckless Tiresias, "she was turned back into a man."

Bottle Rat giggles again.

Knee has a startled and a happy look, his head raised up from his leg. Mockery is a form of homage. Chair Lady has paid him the homage of mocking him. It could be cruelty, kindness, love, a passing joke, encouragement. She's used his knife-chop gesture. She's used it in front of everyone in a signal that, despite appearances, she has all along been paying attention to him. She still does not bother to look in his direction, but his rapture is comical.

Fool, I am thinking. Look at the way she looks

at me. *Me.* I am Odysseus, remember? I am heroic. I am irresistible. I am life. I am blood. And you gave me that respect. Well, I've heard of such things before. Some men, even strident vulnerable assholes, develop a secret groveling respect toward their more successful rivals.

She winks at me. I am sure of it. She looks directly into my eyes for an instant and her eyelid flickers. I feel a twinge, an excitement, a gratitude toward her, a liquid feeling that survives the death-ache of my body and seems to me like proof of the point—I am alive and Knee is nothing. He is a shade of gray.

"Then why am I Tiresias?" Guitar asks.

"Isn't it apropos?" Chair Lady says mildly.

"You think I've taken a few up the ass?" he says.

"Haven't you?" she says.

"Haven't we all?" he says.

"You're trying to turn it into a metaphor," she says, throwing him a subtle wink too. "That's deflection. I meant it literally."

"My hole," he says, strumming a minor seventh, "is protected. Covered by steel strings, you see."

"Your refusal to answer the question answers the question," Knee says sternly. He's seen Chair Lady wink at me and wink at Guitar and so predictably he is cranky again. His rapture is gone.

He is the miserable swain. The more depressed he looks the more he chews.

He is surreptitiously watching Chair Lady.

Chair Lady is surreptitiously watching Guitar.

Guitar, hunched over his instrument, his face half hidden by his long white hair, is surreptitiously watching me.

And I begin to understand some of the threads of the macramé.

The old transsexual is watching me.

He's watching me because I am broken.

I can read it in his eyes.

He sees a human body of a type that is supposed to fit the curves of his brain, but the body is so warped and broken that it can no longer cozy up to any of those curves. And it saddens him. He has spent a lifetime feeling a certain type of nurturing, a type of desire, a type of tenderness, a type of love, and that part of his emotion is squeezed by the sight of me. The sight hurts him. Vulnerability, he says. A condition he knows about. My pelvis being twisty, and his sexuality not generally being considered straight, he and I have an intrinsic similarity. We are companions in otherness.

Chair Lady? Her wink at me was no message to me. How egotistically silly of me. I understand, with a certain bitter taste, that I am not the object of her fascination. Her wink at me was a sideways message to Guitar. She perceives the energy passing from him to me. His empathy is a palpable substance between us like a gelatinous dildo. She tries to understand. Why does this spirited old man, the man she admires—the man she loves maybe?—why does he have such an unexpected compassion for me? That is the problem that occupies her mind and drives her sardonic humor. It worries her.

And Nervous Chewer? He is not jealous of me. I'm nobody. A momentary spectacle. A dying visitor from the world of the living, as he put it with irony and insight. I may drop in for a moment but his world, the Hades of the Central Park homeless, has its own ongoing intrigues and jealousies. The unrequited swain, a nervous fool much smarter than he realizes, wallows in anguish, outcompeted by the allure of Tiresias, a rival he cannot help admiring.

What is love? What is art?

A loves B loves C loves D, and whoever happens to perch in isolation at the top of that dreadful stack must be by definition art.

13

"I'll take the conch," Chair Lady says.

Everything she says hints at mockery. I don't know what she's mocking. Plausibly herself. Her homelessness. Or maybe the other members of the tribunal? The art object of the moment? The absurdity of an elite conversation in rags under a leaky roof? Far from opposites, humor and seriousness have an affinity to each other, and I can see that affinity in the subtle crinkle at the corner of her mouth. Humor and desperation. Humor and that brand of empathy that comes from having little or nothing of your own except cheap glass jewelry and an enigmatic smile.

She reaches out with her foot. She props herself on her elbows on the damp wooden floor, her right leg stretched out, a sneakered foot pointed toward me, her leg so skinny that the fabric of her jeans hangs over the boney scaffold. The canvass sneaker has acid holes and through the holes I can see two of her toes. No socks. Her sneaker touches my chair and gently nudges it, turns me another few degrees with another squeak and another rattle of the rusty metal bearings. The chair tilts slightly and I come to rest facing her directly.

"Why," she says, looking into my eyes, "does a person take everything off, every bit of cloth and showmanship, every pretense, and say please, this is all I have left?

"Dependant arising. In a phrase, that's what it is. Sorry—jargon from my past. We depend on each other to lift ourselves up. Suffering is craving is fear is delusion is clinging to selfhood, clinging to objects, clinging to the trivia that we think makes us happy. Clinging to superficialities. Clinging to the covering that separates us from each other. Strip off all that delusion, and we take a step toward each other and a step toward enlightenment. I don't know, you guys, but I don't see any sculpture here. I don't see art in the discuss-what-it-means sense. I see a person searching for spiritual insight." She looks at me thoughtfully but I don't see anything like insight in her eyes. Curiosity. Dread. For a moment the humor is gone and her eyes are captured entirely by curiosity and dread.

She sits up and rubs her elbows where they were pressed against the floor. I feel a sudden deep sorrow for her elbows. They must have red marks in the shape of the grain of the wood.

The group is silent.

She says, briskly, smiling, "Don't be shy. I can feel the collective distrust."

A meditative "ping, zing," from Guitar.

"Mouthing off about Mahayana Buddhism," she says. "Yawn. Oh dear. Have we come to that again? How embarrassing. She's gone batty."

Knee stirs, looks up, looks around with an apologetic smile. "Our refusal to answer the question answers the question?"

"Thank you," she says.

"I think we're waiting," Cloak explains, "to find out what sophistication lies behind the tantric claptrap."

"Thank *you*," Chair Lady says. "How intellectually phrased. Look at the special contempt you save for spirituality. For any kind of love."

"Maybe I've had so much of love," says Guitar, "one way or the other, as you so delicately pointed out before, that I'm a little embarrassed by it now."

"*I'm* not embarrassed," Bottle Rat says cheerfully.

"I know you're not," Chair Lady says. (She has respect in her voice when she talks to him. I do not yet understand his relationship to the group. I will have to pay attention.)

"The rest of you," she says, scowling, "your minds are in the gutter. You're thinking love as sex. Gross and goofy. Or mushy and sentimental. An easy way to dismiss the topic with a snarky laugh. The worst of the Westernized Tantric fraud. I'm talking about something else."

"What then?" from the chorus.

"This, then," she says. "Here we are together."

"That's love?" says Knee with a hopeful if confused look on his face.

Chair Lady rolls her eyes. "Why are you men so self centered? Love is a group function. All right, it's orgiastic, if you really want. You have no conception of what I'm talking about, do you?" She flashes another comi-serious crinkle at the corner of her mouth. "I'll be more explicit."

With a shake of her head to clear her thoughts of distraction, and to clear her face of wet strands of hair and flecks of water, she begins.

"Buddhism has a lot of variants. I've taught more than two or three of them. I can't vouch for them all. Some of them are more dogmatic

than others. But essential Buddhism, the start-
ing point, the original as I understand it, is a
singularly non-religious religion. 'Believe nothing, no matter where you read it, or who said it,
even if I said it, unless it agrees with your own
reason and your own common sense.' That's a
quote from the Buddha himself. So go away with
your claptrap. Not much claptrap here. One of
the fundamental principles of the thing is, no
claptrap allowed. No demagoguery.

"So go on and flaunt your science at me. I'm
right there looking back at you. I happen to
have a pretty good grounding in topology, thank
you very much, along with a few other scien-
tific topics that might surprise you. Love is too
mushy a thing for you? Spiritual enlightenment
too much like a ghost story? Buddhists were the
first to realize that everything is defined by its
audience. Emptiness, they call it. Each object
is, inside itself, empty. It exists only in relation.
That's a Buddhist insight from more than two
thousand years before the standard model of
physics, which more or less says the same thing.

"So I'll give you that, the audience is important. Our connectivity is important. The naked
man himself, he's also important. His vitality,
sure, absolutely. The deep meaning of this and
that, it's all important. But we're still missing the

fundamental. All this *stuff* we talk about lives inside a space, inside a moment. It *generates* the moment. Think about the moment. Just the moment.

"Or better, to get at the moment, think about how you got here. To this spot, tonight. I was on Fifth Avenue. I know you came from the other side," nodding to Guitar. "I don't know *where* you normally hang during the day," wiggling a shoulder vaguely toward Knee. "I certainly don't know how our visitor got here other than by looming in the front door out of the rain. We each came here on a different path.

"A path is a thread is a story is a plot. You see this, do that, step in a puddle, avoid getting clipped by a taxi, pick a few grimy quarters off the sidewalk, hop around the fast walkers, eat a bagel, scratch an itch on your nose, think something, feel something, do something. Want something. Things happen on your way from A to B. Things happen. That's plot. That's life. That's the minutia of life, anyway. The mechanics of existence. We're chivvied from one event to the next by desire, or accident, or whim, or luck, or stupidity.

"Then we reach a space, here, this little house, this sanctuary, this stillness, this company, this moment, where we can put the plot on hold, and sit down, and have a conversation. How simple is that? A conversation. That's spiritual love. That's when our threads snarl up together."

She lifts her hands and snarls her fingers into her necklaces.

"Love is this space, this literal damp dim wooden dump of a space, this moment, because here we abandon linearity. We abandon plot. We abandon logic. We abandon story altogether. We come in contact with stillness. Love is stillness. Art is Love and Love is a conversation. And by conversation I don't mean the macramé theory. A neat pentagonal web between us? The story of how I think of what you think of what I think? That's not what I see. That's a reductive vision. That's math, as I said before. I see something much more alluring, a tangle, a lovely mess, a pile of spaghetti. That's what we came here for."

"I certainly came here for the spaghetti," Guitar says quietly to the strings of his guitar. Nobody laughs. His offhand joke would seem like disrespect except that, given how skinny he is, how skinny they all are, sticks lost in their plaids and flannels and beads and cloaks, I see more horror than humor in his humor.

Chair Lady flicks a hand toward him, rattling her beads like a shaman exorcising his irreverent thought.

"Shut *up* for a moment. You need to listen to me, all of you, because now I have something to say. You need to be quiet. You need to be patient and stop the sarcastic asides. I'm putting a lid on my own sarcasm and that doesn't happen very often—as you know. I'm telling you about something that's true, that's not just at the center of us as people but at the center of everything we do, think, feel, say, big or trivial.

"You look around. You look at this place. You look at me, our naked guest, the railing, that broken tree, your eyes move from A to B. In motion your eyes see nothing, a blur, a smear, incoherence, that's action, that's narrative, that's drive, that's desire leading you from place to place. Then your eyes come to rest for an instant and the rest allows you to grasp an experience, it allows you the pleasure of holding a little bit of the truth. And you *see*. Art and love and joy and truth are in that moment of stillness. Not in the movement between.

"All right. Again. You pick up a mashed old muddy paperback book that somebody left on a park bench and you give it a try. It's a thriller, a mystery, it has a plot, it moves from A to B to C, it's wonderfully entertaining, it passes the time, but aren't you also disturbed when a book like that distracts you from your own truth? Of course the distraction is why anybody reads the book. It's entertaining. It's easy. But all the commotion in the book is also anesthetizing. In the middle of a page of whosey chasing whatsey you look up and there's sunlight and a leaf on the ground and you're thinking, why am I reading *this*? And plop it goes back on the bench. No wonder it was left in the first place.

"Then again, maybe it's a different book altogether, maybe it's a book that creates its own space, its own truth, its own stillness, its own moment of experience, of emotional experience, or of sensory experience, or of intellectual experience, and then when you look up in the middle of a page, you see the sun, you see the leaf, and for just that instant you're confused because you can't be certain which space is more real: the one around you or the one in the book. Now this is the difference between plot and art. Plot is movement, is action, is sequence, is commotion, is desire to find out what comes next. Art is *now*. Plot and art are antithetical. The only artistic use of plot is to entice you step by step along a path, and so lead you unexpectedly into a place where linearity ends, where a conversation can happen, where meaning has a chance."

Chair Lady takes a deep breath.

"Sorry. Carried away. You all know what I'm

telling you. I'm not even telling you as much as reminding you. It's intrinsic to us. It's *in* us as people. We can't help knowing it. If our guest stands for anything—and I don't honestly think he does—then he stands for the one aesthetic lesson. The more we theorize about him, the farther we get from the truth. He isn't a sculpture. He isn't a peg that holds up yarn. He isn't data for a theory. And he isn't a bucket of blood. Except in the most literal sense. He's a human being. The bizarreness of his appearance jiggles our brains. Makes us talk. Gives us an excuse. Good for us. But at the same time, look at how worried he is. I can see it in his face. He came here on invitation and sat down and kindly kept his mouth shut and his eyes open. His politeness to us is overwhelming. He doesn't stand for something. He isn't art. The *moment* is art, as much as any other moment if we let it be that way. He's a part of the moment. Think about the aesthetic personality of the moment. The sheer bizarreness, which is to say the uniqueness, of us, where we are, as we are. The nowness of now. You've heard of seize the day. I say love the moment. Look at us, and look at him, and look at how we are."

14

Chair Lady says no more. Having taken a risk and exposed her earnestness, a part of her that she evidently views as a vulnerability, she is penitent now, hands folded under her necklaces, eyes thoughtfully on that hole in the toe of her sneaker. She nods once as to say, "Go on, somebody take the conch from me."

"I already went," mumbles Knee.

"Same," says Cloak.

"My turn?" says Guitar.

I wonder if he'll try to one-up Chair Lady. The challenge of the committee. Each member tries to out-do the last. Each perspective is more subtle, more cosmic, at the same time more personal. How can he hope to compete with the poetry of her version? I feel a glow of appreciation for her anti-theoretic theory that humanizes me without having to say one word about who I am as a human.

Guitar watches me. I can't see his eyes; only the shadow in his sockets. He seems to be contemplating me, sorting his philosophical options. I've already sensed his empathy for me, and I wonder if he will try to put it to words or leave it assumed and choose a different topic entirely.

"Art," says Guitar.

Ping!

"Theory One. Art is something nailed up for public amusement. With strings that attach its arms and legs to the members of the audience. We pull the strings and it dances?"

He holds up a hand toward Cloak to stop any argument. "My view of your view of our view of art."

Ping!

"Theory two. Art feeds us the blood of life. Which has some thematic relationship to the first theory. Reminds me of crucifixion anyway, as much as of Homer or Dante or Prince Vlad."

Ping!

"Theory three. Art is the love of a moment. Except it isn't a theory but a truth without a concept. An actuality, maybe. And I'll accept that art can be love. But I don't know if that makes it the harshest theory of them all so far, because love is so very harsh. It can be."

Ping.

"Theory four—"

He shakes his head, then begins to strum. He plays a little tune and the tune is cheerful with a dance step, but in the silence and the rain and the darkness and the philosophical ambiguity, the cheerfulness feels more like a lost thought. The fragility of the tune is disquieting.

"I'm going to have to go with something un-popular," he says, ending the tune abruptly be-fore the final cadence. "Art? It's killing me."

He bows his head to let his white-gray hair trail over the guitar. He lifts his head, looks up, far up, bends his neck back until I can see his narrow throat and gristly Adam's apple, bits of gray hair straggling out of it. He sighs and shakes his head.

Everyone is silently respectful of Breezy Tir-eezy.

"All art is failure. But I mean that in an op-timistic sense. I'm sorry for the contradiction. Our guest brings that platitude so much to life that I can't stand it. All art is failure."

He picks up his jaunty tune, then breaks off again.

On the verge of speaking he suddenly changes his mind, launches into a drumming extravaganza, drumming with the flat of his hand on the wooden flat of the guitar, drumming with his shoes on the wooden floor, drumming with his tongue on the front of his teeth, drumming interlocking rhythms, his body in a jerky motion seized by crazed frustration. The music is spiky and astonishing. He stops abruptly and laughs, a little out of breath.

"I'm a musician. A failed musician. But that's redundant, you see. All artists fail. If you don't fail then you aren't trying. I believe that.

"I'm not talking about public success, which is a bore. Or monetary success, which is a sin. That's my creed. Look at me. I can play in the subway and people toss me spare change. Sometimes I'm lucky and get a dollar bill. My clothes smell too much for me to get a gig in a coffee shop anymore. That's the truth. I know—it's easy and convenient, when you're broke and homeless, to brag about your contempt for money. But I am not lying. If I had wanted money I would have at least given it a try. I never had that lust. I was too busy. I was busy my whole life chasing aesthetic success. Reaching that aesthetic goal? You never do. You try. You push. You put your back up against a cathedral and try to move it.

"Can you imagine? The people walking by and mocking you? *What* are you doing, Idiot? And there you are, scratched and bleeding from the friction on brick and stone and concrete. You're thirsty, starving, exhausted, your muscles are cramping. Push with your shoulder for a while, switch off to the other shoulder, then your chest, then both hands braced on the wall, then head down, pushing with the bone in your forehead against solid brick until the tears run out your eyes. A ridiculosity. A flailing idiot. A buffoon hopping up and down. Sound and fury, as the man said. Well, you try everything and you fail. You fail publically. You give everything to that wall. You give it yourself. And you fail. You know you failed and yet you keep trying because you can't leave it alone. That's lunacy.

"If you're Mozart, then you move the cathedral an inch. One inch. And not a lot of people notice at the time. You're still the butt of the same sneering attitude, the neglect, the contempt of those who think they know better. And you have two conflicting ideas in your head. One is, I did it. I actually moved this damn thing an inch. It's possible! And it's exhilarating! And you appreciate your own worth; because who else can move a cathedral? But at the same time you have precisely the opposite thought. *One inch?* That's it?

That's the limit of my ability? That's not success. That's failure. I have failed.

"I've succeeded. I've failed.

"No contradiction there. The easy way those two realizations can snuggle up against each other is horrifying.

"Every artist dies bragging outwardly but with a lot of bruised organs on the inside.

"All art is failure.

"After you're dead someone might, *might* come along with a measuring tape and say, by God, he got that thing an inch to the North! And then you're famous. Then you're Mozart. Much good it does you, given that you died a failure. Mozart. Schubert. There's a guy who died a failure. Beethoven. He moved his cathedral an inch and a quarter, was an insufferable braggart about it apparently, but died knowing in his heart all about his own failure to do what he wanted to do. I'm mentioning composers because that's what I know. That's what I studied."

The first eight notes of the Ode to Joy plucked out on the guitar.

"Why a cathedral? Why not pick a project of a more convenient size? You can put your back up against a Toyota camry in neutral, and lo! And behold! It moves! How deliciously easy! Or if you like even more convenience, you can lean up against a shopping cart. Something with wheels, you know. Something designed by an engineer to be moved. Move it here! Move it there! Move it all over the parking lot! Frighten the K-Mart shoppers! Get onto the evening news! Product endorsements will follow!

"Why sweat art when you can do something mainstream, something prepared, something arranged for you ahead of time, something less idiotically impossible, something that has a chance at actual public success? It may or may not be art—that's debatable—but it's a lot more economically sensible.

"Sorry. I don't mean to despise the easy approach. It isn't even easy. It takes a lot of work. It's *challenging* to succeed at the mainstream. I never tried, but I hear it is. What I mean is, for all the hard work, it does have its own comfort. It has the advantage of clear definition. You don't need to wonder if you've gone plain stark idiotically crazy mad, pushing, pushing in a direction nobody else sees or cares about.

"Art doesn't have that comfort. Art wears you out. The part that wears you out is the mental resistance, the emotional resistance, the self doubt, of tackling a building that the rest of the world already accepts as it is, as something that belongs here, as something rooted in place, and here you come along pushing on it and trying to move it out from under the congregation. And the congregation doesn't even notice the crazy guy outside pushing on the building. Why should it? An artist is an ineffectual idiot.

"Just how big a cathedral do you need to tackle, anyway, before you can fairly call it art? If a shopping cart doesn't qualify, what does, and how will you recognize it when you see it? Am I expected to murder myself against a Mozart-sized edifice, or would something smaller be sufficient for me to feel that I've gained the status of artist? What's fair? If fairness has any relevance, which I think it does not.

"Now that I'm old and hoary and wise and breezy I have a good guess at the answer to that question: simply this: if you know in your heart that you failed, then it might actually be art. If you think you succeeded, then you didn't try for something big enough and you didn't attain art."

He drums again, a blur of hands and shoes in the dim light, a racket of bangs and booms and slaps and yelps of enthusiasm.

He stops mid drum and laughs.

"A self-confirming theory. I know I am an artist because I am a failure. And therefore I'm a success. But isn't it true? What kind of joy could

I get sitting in a stretch limo sipping my little pinky martini and insisting, insisting, insisting that I'm a musical genius—wondering if my real talent might after all lie in the mundane art of insisting instead of the high art of music? No. Here I am. Here I am."

He drums again, his hair flying around his face, his guitar ringing and echoing.

"You," stopping again and nodding to Chair Lady, "you're a novelist. I mean aside from your brief self-contradictory stint as a short-tempered Buddhist teacher. I hereby label you a novelist. Listen to you obsessing over narrative and literary spaces. What else could you be? And you," nodding to Cloak, "you trace mathematical patterns. It's okay—even if you are a scientist, you're obsessed by the science of aesthetics. An artist, one way or the other. And you," nodding to Knee, "a culinary artist of the most exquisite and unusual fare. Or a scholar of epic poetry. Or a phenomenologist of the drug culture. More that last one, I think. An artist, all the same. I have you all pegged. Artists. All artists. Look at us artists. Look at us failures. Under a leaky roof in last month's clothes, starving. We are the elite of artistic success."

He gestures toward me with the neck of the guitar.

"Our friend? He is the personification, but the living *image*, of art as failure. That's my new placard for him. An artist. Broken, stripped, exposed, damaged, ruined—an artist. An artist, I said to myself when I looked at him. Think of the brashness it takes to strip off and say, Hey World, here I am! Me. Not my covers. Take a look at *me* if you dare. I'm ruined and I'm ugly and anyone can see it who dares to look. An artist. An artist. An artist's performance art depicting the art of being an artist."

15

"Now!" says Guitar, putting aside his instrument and getting to his feet. He strides to me in two steps, takes hold of the back of the chair and spins me to face the opposite direction as easily as if I were sitting in a shopping cart. For a moment I feel dizzy.

"Go ahead," he says. "He's all yours. Best for last."

I'm facing Bottle Rat. He has been quiet, contributing only a comment here and there, and now I see why. He's been nibbling. He looks like a rodent interrupted in the middle of its meal, a seed between its two forepaws. In his hands, at fingertips, he is holding a green bottle cap in the beginning stages of dental fray.

"Oh but I'm cheating," he says nervously. "I talked to him already. I'm, you know, contaminated by what he told me."

"That's okay," says Cloak respectfully. I'm surprised to hear respect coming from that source.

"Tell us what you think," says Chair Lady, encouragingly.

Knee's large eyes are fixed in fascination on Bottle Rat.

The committee is expectant. I catch a whiff of hero warship that I do not yet understand.

"I liked talking to him," Bottle says. "I thought he was nice. He said he went naked because of existential polyester on his skin that gave him a rash. I mean, that's the gist of it. Not exactly his words. He was running around and I watched him sit on a bench next to the lake. So I went up and said hi, you know, and I—"

Here he stops abruptly and returns to his chewing. He teases out a bit of plastic, bites with great delicacy using his incisors while his audience waits, then spits an invisible fleck of plastic onto the floor at his side.

"I heard him hollering about killing somebody. I really liked him from the start. Before I could tell he was naked. You can't see that well in the park in the evening, and I just saw him looming along sort of and shouting. You know

how everyday the park fills u
And they're never really int
kind of strange. Why aren't
those jugglers and perform
spiked hair people and, yo
down skateboarders that
and, and Frisbee showo...

Anyway then here's a guy who I can tell rig--
away I think he's really neat. He's one of us. I
don't know how. Twisty naked man. Like a twisty
naked oak root sticking out of the path. It's—"

Another long silence while he chews on the
green bottle cap.

"And," he says, then pauses to spit with a po-
lite precision, the tip of his tongue sticking out.
"He wasn't drunk either. You can smell that. He
is what he is. Which is . . . Well, I think it's just—"

The audience remains attentive through his
pauses.

I don't sense that Mr. Rat is aiming toward a
point. He has no discernable theory of art. He's
rambling while his attention is fixed on his work.

And suddenly I understand why he is treated
with such hushed respect.

He is the logical final step in the one-ups-man-
ship. Each member of the group has put forward
a theory and tried, confusedly, to articulate the
truth of art. Now never mind the theories, the

e effort, the desperate human compul-
to explain. Bottle Rat *lives* art. He has no
ed to explain. He is what each of us wishes we
could be and that we know we will never be. He
breaks our hearts.

He's creating another bird. I can see the tail
taking shape. The workmanship is so perfect
that I can already recognize the overlapping tail
feathers of a mourning dove.

The others aren't listening to the words.
They're watching sculpture coming out of his
mouth. The talent is a natural phenomenon,
like Mozart, like da Vinci, inexplicable and so astonishing that all the minor envies and sarcasms
people normally pass among each other in a
conversation become meaningless. We are awed.

How's this for art, if I can spin my own theory
in my own mind and keep my mouth shut.

Something unexpected. Something simple. A
bird. A plastic bird in such lovely detail that you
cannot believe it without seeing it. It makes you
feel protective. It makes you feel sad for its vulnerability and glad for its existence. It renders
reasons and arguments irrelevant. It renders
you, your own self, your own awful predicament,
irrelevant. In the moment that you look at it you
see it and that is enough.

But at the same time that it takes you away

from yourself, it also reminds you of yourself, because we're all throw-away bits of plastic chewed up into our individual shapes.

I bet they go for about a buck fifty.

Each one is distilled. It is tiny. The efficiency of the package is a part of its quality. Do the people who buy them have any idea what they've got? If you could collect them and arrange them in a museum in a glass case, if you could convince a curator to display something so odd made of such garbage and carved with such a primal tool, if you could convince patrons to stop in their bored amble through the museum and notice them, would anyone recognize them for what they are?

But it isn't that kind of art. It isn't made for institutional fame. Public appreciation is unlikely and irrelevant. Bottle Rat simply chews them and dispenses them, and the plastic birds are the same either way.

16

"I see a light," says Knee.

Bottle Rat looks up from his nibbling with a smile and peers. All heads turn. They look between the wooden balusters of the railing. Sitting higher on my chair I can see over the top of the railing.

A light is bobbing. A flashlight? I hear boots crackling through dead bracken. Just enough moonlight filters through the rain clouds, just enough city light reflects from the undersides of the clouds, that I can see down a hill, a steep muddy bank covered in sparse bushes, to the lumps of rock rising out of the mud, to a gravel path, to the smear of a better lighted part of the park.

A beam of light transfixes the gazebo, then flicks away again.

The committee whispers.

"Is it coming closer?"

"Who is it?"

"Police?"

"What do you see?"

The footsteps approach.

In a scramble, a skitter, like insects pouring over a log, the members of the Central Park Philosophical Homeless Art Explication Club jump to a hands-and-feet crouch, rush the railing, climb it and drop to the wet ground on the far side of the gazebo. Chair Lady's beads swing for an instant, catching the light, rattling, and then she is gone over the side. Knee's eyes are filled with anguish and fear, his chin jiggling. Guitar has one hand clamped around the neck of his intrument—it bumps the wooden railing with a resonant jangle. The guitar will suffer in the rain. Cloak's dark fabric billows over the railing and disappears into the night. Bottle Rat grins. He looks excited by the diversion, lets out a shrill giggle, stuffs the green beginning of a mourning dove into his front left pocket, the opposite pocket to the red bird, and scrambles after the others. He hops the railing and disappears.

Splashes, thuds on the muddy ground, silence.

The shades have disappeared into the forest.

I am too cold, too sick, too achy to move, and so here I remain. Sitting on a rattling old metal office chair. Sitting naked in the middle of a wooden gazebo in the middle of the park at night. I am cold, and I am alone, and I *still* haven't learned who or what I am, and a heavy drop of water falls on the top of my head.

The beam of the flashlight transfixes me. For a long moment it and I stare each other down. I am absolutely silent. I don't breathe. I don't dare to shiver. I'm too startled to be afraid. I'm too confused to remember what terror is anymore, even though my heart is racing and my mouth has gone dry. Maybe the police have caught up with me at last for matricide. Maybe I deserve it.

17

When the light switches off and releases my vision, I see a policeman standing just outside the structure leaning and staring in, his arms crossed over the broad wooden top of the railing, one sinewy hand dangling inside in a casual gesture. He and I watch each other.

"Vagrancy," he says.

He shakes his head. He has a gravelly voice, a police voice. I'm not sure he can see my whole body clearly. For all he can tell I might be in shorts or swimming trunks, admittedly an odd fashion choice for the season.

"I could pick you up on vagrancy," he says. "I could pick up the others too. You're new to the group." He peers at me in curiosity.

I've gotten used to the condition of mutism. I maintain voice silence. I watch him; he watches me.

"Sorry about the light," he says. "Hope I didn't blind you too bad."

I shake my head.

"They all run away just now?" he says.

I nod.

"I thought I heard them trampling off. They always do. You're not very talkative tonight, are you?"

"I haven't spoken in a few hours," I explain, my voice sounding strange to me. "They asked me not to."

"Sure. I see. You're not part of the group yet. They had you in as a silent guest."

"That's right," I say, surprised. "How did you know?"

"Oh I know all about them," he says. "If I come here with my light on, they run like crazy. They think I'll bust them. I never do. Sometimes I sneak up in the dark, crouch right around here next to the house, and listen in on them. Better than TV, you know. Crazy idiots, but very smart." He nods his head sharply. "They wouldn't ever let *me* sit in the middle. That's a sure thing."

I didn't expect a policeman to be wistful about a group of vagrants. "You'd like to join in?" I ask in amazement.

"Sometimes, sure."

"You couldn't come in plain clothes?"

"Dress like a homeless? No. They know my face already. No, the only way I can join is by hiding in the shadows."

"I'm sorry they won't accept you."

He shrugs his cop-broad shoulders. "It is what it is. Exclusion, you know? It isn't just for the rich anymore." He smiles at his joke. "How did they end up including you? That's unusual. That's an honor, I'd say."

"The little one, Bottle Rat, he found me sitting on a bench and invited me in. They were trying to figure out what I am. Or what I stand for."

He nods, impressed, eyebrows arched. "I wish I could have heard that conversation. What did they decide? What are you?"

"Art, mostly," I tell him. "Apparently. I'm flattered. I'm definitely part of a larger picture. But they couldn't agree on what exactly art is."

"That's usual," he says. "I love that conversation. Theories of art. You want to know my theory?"

I'm not certain I do. I've been beaten up by five theories already.

"Don't worry," he says. "Mine is easy. Well it's more a theory of *them*. They're not talking about art, really. They're so bad off, being homeless and hard up, they like to put a kind of a separation between themselves and everything else in life. Pretend they're sitting back at a distance and watching it. Discussing it. Feels safer that way."

"That sounds plausible," I say. "But art or life, whatever you want to call it, I admit I was hoping they'd talk less about themselves and more about me in specific."

He winks at me, lifts a finger to swipe the side of his nose, and says, "There is no you. Didn't you realize that?"

A laugh startles out of me. "I think you're right. I like that."

I am my own understanding. My understanding is of them. Ergo, understanding them, I exist as them. That last phrase I accidentally utter out loud.

"Goddam," he says. "You've been listening to them too much. You don't want to sound like a lunatic."

"Then how would you put it?" I ask.

"I wouldn't put it. Sometimes it's better not to think so much about how to say things. I have the graveyard shift all night in the park, and I walk around with my flashlight and my cuffs and mace and this and that, and I have to put in a lot of hours that could feel spooky if I thought too hard. But if I just look and listen, and see the darkness, and feel the rain, and breathe the cold, and hear the ground under my feet, and smell the mud, and sure, listen in on a deep conversation or two, then I'm okay. I'm alive. That's all I need. I'll show you something."

He fishes into the front pocket of his shirt with two fingers and pulls out—a coin maybe? A memento? A charm, I think. He holds it toward me on the palm of his hand.

It's a Bottle Rat bird.

"That shows you who I am," he says. "It sums it up, pretty much. Most amazing thing. I want to know: what's the address of the Manhattan School of Tooth Bird Method Sculpture Thing? It's damn crazy. Plain amazing." He puts the bird away reverently in his shirt pocket as though returning his soul to his body cavity. "I've kept this little guy safe all year. You want to know who that man is? I'm on to him."

"Who is he?"

"God. That's who. I figure God's a creative guy. So when he comes down and lives with us in disguise, he can't help leaking creations here and there."

"God?"

"God. Either that or he's an idiot. I haven't decided yet. Not a normal idiot—an idiot savant. God, idiot savant, what's the difference?"

"That's very deep," I tell him, a little skeptically.

"You think it over," he says. "You'll see I'm right."

He checks his watch.

"I need to hit the main path. You want my coat? You look pretty much exposed to the cold."

"I'm naked," I tell him, in case he hasn't entirely realized.

"Vagrancy *and* public indecency. You *are* a menace to society. It's a good thick wool," he adds, tugging on the lapel of his police blazer.

"I'm okay," I tell him.

"Suit yourself." He spurts out a snort of laughter at his unintended joke. "So to speak. Maybe I'll see you again, Naked Art Object."

Before leaving he hesitates, grimaces, looks intently up at the dark underside of the roof, avoiding my face, and says, "A word to the wise. Call's out for a naked man who snatched off a lady's ipod and tossed it over a wall. That wouldn't be you, would it?"

"A what? Sorry? What? A lady who what?"

He winks at the ceiling and says nothing.

"I . . . no. Is the lady all right?"

"Seems to be," he says.

"She didn't go over the wall?"

"Not that I heard. She ran and got her property back, and was all around more worried about the guy."

"I . . . but no, I had a. . . ."

Now he unfixes his eyes from the ceiling and watches me closely. "Tell you what. I've just had a chance to chat with you, a good long chat, and in my opinion, you can't be that man, because you're not deranged. The report specifically mentioned a *deranged* naked man. You're a mentally together, calm, intellectual kind of a naked park original. Must be an anarchist. Or an artist. One of those. Am I right?"

"Sure. I think so."

"Of course I'm right. Now, you go put on some clothes. You don't have to be naked to be an artist, do you? It confuses people. It'll cause you trouble. Why do you want to break the rules and cause so much trouble? Get dressed and go home for the night. Pay the rules a little respect. I have to tell you that anyway, because it's my job. But now that we got it out of the way, let me tell you something even more important." He wags a finger at me. "Don't take the rules too seriously."

Nodding, he turns and makes his way energetically across the soggy lawn, his flashlight switched on, the circle of light bobbing along the ground in front of him.

For a long time I sit with my hands folded in my lap and think about the simplicity of redemption.

Is it possible to be redeemed for a sin that never occurred? How can I feel so confused, and so relieved, because of an event that happened only in my imagination?

Of course the woman never fell over the wall. How stupid of me. Otherwise the police would have acted differently and I would be in jail now. Nobody cared to rescue a woman who was pushed into traffic? Nobody handcuffed me? Nobody guarded me or stopped me as I limped away? I was too befuddled to see the absurdity. Now my head is clearer. How trivially the whole worry has disappeared. And how good breathing feels, even though the air smells just as much like mud and damp lumber as it did two minutes ago. I see now that I've done nothing to be forgiven, admired, despised, condemned, or celebrated. My fundamental assumptions were wrong. Evidently I know nothing. I've done nothing. I've hurt nobody. I've accomplished nothing either bad or good. I'm worth nothing. I simply am. I exist. And I don't mind. I am finding a satisfying liberty in that humble status.

18

What is the relationship between art and life?

I don't mean anything as dull as art imitates life or life imitates art. As though life lives in this house and art lives down the block in that house, and sometimes they steal each other's interior decoration designs. Art imitates art, for that matter, and life imitates life. Everything imitates everything, and despite the imitation, somehow everything seeks to find its own intrinsic personality. Or failing that, is absorbed and has no meaning.

No, what I mean is that all bits of life are, in themselves, of their own essence, bits of art. And art, as traditionally imagined, is merely those bits of life that somebody decided to collect and put in a display case.

I mean that art and life are the same substance. You can talk about them using different vocabulary, but the vocabulary distracts, confuses, and when the words are stripped away, what is left but the same essence?

A more roundabout, but more thorough way to explain my thought is that the human metaphor engine is infinitely capable. We can make anything become a metaphor for anything. Any happenstance, any string of events, any picture, any sound, any accident of life, any random moment, can loom in the mind as suffused with meaning, as a representation of the cosmos or of a cracked fingernail. The reason for this deep metaphorical connectivity between any X and any Y, however cosmic or trivial the X or the Y, is that everything contains the same essential property. Everything shares a fundamental.

I am talking about the warmth of human awareness. What it feels like for this moment to be this moment. The nowness of now. The truth of the smell of wet decaying oak leaves on the ground in the park at night. Awareness has a joy to it such that every moment you experience, no matter how lovely or horrible, is palpably beautiful. Because all things in experience are suffused with the same beauty of awareness, all things are in that way interchangeable. Because all things are interchangeable, all things can stand as metaphors for each other. Because all things are metaphors for all things, art exists.

Poetry at its poorest, which is to say life at its poorest, is a metaphor so limited that it can't fit more than two items in its vision at a time. It tries to convince you cleverly, intellectually, that a specific X is a specific Y. A cross-word-puzzle allegory. A game of what does this mean? What does that mean? What does it *stand* for, man? Give me the answer key.

The richest art, the richest moment in life, is an open metaphor. It doesn't try to convince you of anything. It holds itself as a candle. The light spreads and illuminates anything in the world of experience, anything you choose to look at in the glow of that particular candle. The choice is yours.

Listen to me thinking. Every experience is art. Every moment glows with meaning and has the potential to illuminate every other moment. How convenient. Maybe a dying person will always arrive at the same conclusion. Because what else can I say to myself? What do I have left? Look to the future, and it's empty. Look to the logic of the world, and it will have to hold together or fall apart without me. Look to my ambitions, and they seem mighty irrelevant all of a sudden. Look to the people important to me, or to the people I used to imagine were important to me, and they will have to make do on their own. The only reassurance left to me is the knowledge that I've had my own collection of moments, that they were strong enough and gorgeous enough to sustain me, and that I still have one or two moments to go.

Closing in on the end is itself an experience. It may be bitter but it is also potent. The quality of metaphor runs through it. A final night in the park can represent anything I wish, illuminate anything I choose to see. A crazy jumble of events, illogically scattered, sorts itself in my mind and forms a dozen possible narratives. Which narrative will I choose for myself?

To me the night is a recapitulation. It is the trajectory of my life.

It is an epic in the true Aristotelian sense: a small piece that stands for the larger whole. A few weeks in the last year of the war. And so the fate of the universe is illuminated.

The trajectory of a life starts and you don't know why. You don't know why you came into the business naked, equipped with nothing of value, only a stinky amniotic slipperiness and death like a germinating peach pit already inside your abdomen.

You pretend that you did the whole trick to yourself on purpose, but what the purpose may be, you can't quite say.

You wander, you want to show the world what you are, you screw up, you out-and-out kill the people who nurture you, you use them up, you are lost in culpability, you are lost in emotion, you are lost in darkness, you rely on sheer sophomoric audacity and on chance and you find a place for yourself. That place is a conversation that can sustain you for a while, a collaborative effort to pull ourselves up by the shoestrings, or heartstrings, or conversational strings. A conversation lifts us all into abstraction, saves us for a while from the dirt and the pain and the mud and the darkness and the failure and the reality, even if those things are themselves the topics of the conversation. A conversation creates a space and you live in that space. You *are* the people in the conversation. For a while they define you. You are a him and a her and another, you *are* the jerk and you *are* the lover and you *are* God. You see more because you see through other people's eyes. You see yourself through other people's eyes. But a good conversation, at the same time that it lifts you up, wears you down, and at the same time that it teaches you about yourself, it distracts you from your own experience, and at the same time that it encourages you to love, it contra-poses people, and at the same time that you are put into words for the idiotic purpose of immortalizing yourself to the people who aren't even listening to you, you are watching your own life pass by.

Strange that it all seems so important at the time. All those *ideas*. Intellectualism. Philosophy. Dogma. Ideology. Positions defined and elaborated and litigated, digressions and addenda, clever ironies and righteous certitude. *Progress*. The world depends on it. Society will collapse if we don't engage. Your life has finally plugged itself into a larger conversation and you are a busy part of it.

Then the conversation is over and you realize how dull it was. What the heck was all that junk? Nobody really said anything. Nothing depended on it. No insight was gained. No progress. Ideas, intellectualism, yes, plenty of that. But the positions mush into each other and none of them matter. In retrospect it seems like a giant boring swath of useless complexity that took up the largest share of effort in a life. You begin to develop the queasy realization that the purpose of the conversation was merely to distract. To pass the time.

When the conversation ends, when the people who shared that space with you scatter and you realize that you are alone, when you realize that the companionship was an illusion, or maybe an abstraction, and that you have always been alone, and that there is no other possible state except being alone, as harsh as that moment of realization may be, in among the many other emotions, you can't help feeling relief. The complexity is over. The ambiguity is over. The end is here. The final experience is honest. It is simple. It has a personal relationship to you that nothing else can have. Your end is, of its essence, yours and no one else's.

I've heard people claim that they would like to die peacefully during a deep sleep. I wonder if this claim comes from too casual an inspection of the problem. If I must have a last experience, I would like it to be a potent one that escapes anesthesia—whether a literal anesthesia trickling into the vein at the crook of my elbow, or the mental anesthesia of an intellectual snowjob, a clever analysis, a rationalization, academic deconstructing, academic reconstructing. I want my awareness to be as vivid as I can make it. If it is to be horror, let it be horror. If it is to be pain, let it be pain. Let the rats pull my guts out. The experience itself should be an amazed, hysterical, fearful joy. I would like to take off the protective layers and feel the world, see it, smell it, hear it, taste it. I want to seize whatever little bit more I can get.

An idiot's refusal to accept his end. Like a book that keeps petering on after the plot is complete. Yes, yes, I'm sure that's true. I'm sure it's indecent. All the same, however meaningless the scraps at the end may be, I will take what I can get. When I can no longer heave myself into a new moment, that's when I'll stay seated meekly with my hands crossed in my lap like Saint Naked beatified. Right now the silence of this abandoned gazebo is beginning to spook me and I'd like to get up and try again.

19

I try to stand.

I try, but now I'm on the floor. My legs don't seem to work anymore. I'm too numb to feel the impact of my palms and knees on the planking. My arms are trembling as if about to break at the elbows, but I can maintain the quadrupedal pose. I'm good. I'm not dead yet. I have some muscle capacity. I can crawl, anyway.

20

I've crawled a long way through the grass.

The gazebo is a lump of darkness behind me and my existence there, hours of conversation, a microcosm, a whole life of experience it seems, is gone, and now I'm crouching on an asphalt footpath in a new moment of reality in a circle of light. The metal lamppost is icy against my cheek.

A soggy paper sign is taped to the lamppost. Used espresso machine $30.

I feel less alone now because I am on a path and a path leads to places and places contain people.

21

I've dragged myself half a mile farther down the path.

Dawn is approaching. I know because I see an ice cream vendor pushing his wooden cart slowly up the path toward me.

I'm sitting on the ground beside a bench. I must look quite casual, relaxing in the mud and pachysandra as if I had meant to strike exactly this pose. I'd sit on the bench, but I can't get up. I tried.

I watch the ice cream cart approach. Its little metal wheels make a din. Its canvas umbrella, sun-faded red, folded, sticking straight up, wobbles like the mast of a catboat. First it's visible under a lamppost, then obscure, then visible under the next light, then obscure, and so it marks slow time as it approaches me.

As the cart passes my bench, the man pushing it sees me and stops abruptly. He's poised like a superhero, leaning forward, both hands outstretched and braced against the back of his cart. He peers. He pulls his head back, blinks at me, pushes his head forward, blinks again, and I smile at him, but my smile is probably wan.

"You, um, all right?" he says.

"Yes."

"You look hurt."

"I'm comfter-ful."

"You need help? You want an ice cream?"

"No thank you."

"Are you sure?" He seems surprised that I would turn down an ice cream. "You need an ambulance?"

"Absolutely not."

I can hear pugnacity in my voice. I've raised myself almost onto my knees. I didn't realize I had that much energy left in my body.

"It's okay," he says, pulling his head back and blinking again. "You don't have to go anywhere if you don't want to."

For a moment he looks at his cart and then looks back at me in doubt. "You want me to just *leave* you here?"

"I don't mind."

He pauses for a long time with an anxious grimace.

"If you want anything," he says finally, "like an ice cream, I'm just down the path a little way."

22

The exact moment of dawn is always hard to spot, especially when the ground breathes out steam after a winter rain.

A dark quick movement against the gray of the sky—a few birds fluttering.

The landscape has been visible for a while. I suddenly notice that I've gradually been looking at it. I hear rattling vender's carts, rattling dumpsters, footsteps on gravel, out of sight, distant and near, an echogram of the park. The rain stopped more than an hour ago and the day is likely to be sunny.

I survived the night.

I'm resting on the ground, my head on my arms, my arms draped and angled over the wooden seat of the bench beside me, my legs sprawled into the path, my body hair clumped, soaked, clinging to my skin, chilled, my skin gray and mud-spotted.

I shouldn't stay here. I don't want to be found by the morning crowd, reported, apprehended, rescued. Especially rescued. I am afraid of an IV drip, of laundered bedclothes and glowing indicator lights and gently beeping equipment and hushed voices and politeness. I am afraid of the false comfort of anesthesia. The fear is so deep, so irrational, so immediate, that I can neither doubt it nor examine it.

I am not afraid of death (I insist to myself with bravado).

If I stay in the park throughout the day, would the crowds be so cruel and interfering as to rescue a naked wanderer? Or would I blend in? Another freak in the daily parade? I could tell fortunes. I could do magic tricks with donated coins and keep the coins for a living. I could juggle with acorns that I pick up off the ground. I could sit on a bench and draw caricatures for a dollar a-piece. Aren't I an artist? I could use my novelty to attract custom. Mommy, can I get my picture drawn by the Naked Weird Portraitist? Can I?

All fantasies. I am spent. I can't even stand

up. I can't juggle (never could anyway). I can't think straight enough to tell a clever fortune. I can't hold a pencil firmly enough to draw the oval outline of a face and I never will again.

In a moment of pure existential startle I catch myself thinking, what, this is for real?

I'm *done*?

My only choice left is to crawl away and hide?

Maybe up this slope behind the bench, into the dogwood. Quickly, before I'm discovered.

A panic seizes me.

It's time for me to leave the path.

Leave the path?

The double meaning makes me smile and I am glad I still have the capacity to appreciate irony and to appreciate appreciating. However wobbly the corners of my mouth may be.

I scrape myself up the slope through the pachysandra, pulling myself forward on my elbows and the boney blade of my good hip. The stems of the dogwood bush, thin, whippy, clustered densely, rise and curve back down to form a low wicker roof. A cave. A hiding place.

For all my physical weakness, the ache that's finally now transcended any cold-induced numbness, the pain of bones loose in their muscles, the pain of broken internal machinery—let me tell you about pain, the pain of resting my arms

on the seat of a nearby bench for an hour, then
stirring, moving, finding dents in my flesh where
the rivets were pressed into me, and feeling my
thick sluggish blood trickling into those emp-
tied places—the rotting smell of my skin (a foul
smell is itself a horrific visceral type of pain), the
smell of urine and disintegrating kidney that's
seeped out of me and mixed with the drizzle and
oozed onto the path, the psychological pain of
seeing the gray mottled color of my hands and
feet and the tumor standing out horrible and
lumpy against the shriveling of my body—for all
that, for all that it shocks me (how did I arrive at
this awful state so quickly? I wasn't this way at the
start of the night!), for all that I hate my body as
spoiled meat, at the same time I am not cranky
about the trajectory that got me here or about
the place that I've reached. I don't feel resentment. I don't have that option. I'm surprised by
the pragmatism of my emotions. I feel what I
need to feel where I am. I feel as though none of
it is real. I feel as though it is all more real than
anything that has ever happened to me before.
I feel calm. Under the calm I feel queasy. I feel
a jittery panicked triumph. Triumph because I
was true to myself and had the confidence to
get myself here at the end of all things, under a
bush where nobody has ever died before, and to

make it my own bush and my own little dogwood cave. It smells familiar to me. The wet ground looks familiar. The texture of half decayed twigs against my cheek feels familiar. *Everything* has an aura of the familiar. This space and this moment belong to me as if they were an extension of myself. I can't tell anymore where my skin ends and the soggy leaves begin, or where my fingers and toes separate from the wedges of light falling through the branches. I'll spend an hour, if that long, listening to the morning crowd. I know how noisy the park can be. Hundreds of people might trample past my hiding place in the next hour. I can already hear people talking, chatting, gabbling, laughing, and their voices feel like they are rising up from inside me. Solitude and sociality are fused.

THE AUTHOR

Drawing by Wurge

Michael S. A. Graziano, Ph.D., is a professor of Psychology at Princeton University. When not doing research Michael spends his time writing fiction and composing music. He lives in Princeton, N.J., with his family.

About the Type

This book was set in ITC New Baskerville.™ This type-face family is a modern interpretation of the original types cut in 1762 by British type founder and printer John Baskerville. During the centuries since its creation, Baskerville has remained one of the world's most widely used typefaces.

Designed by John Taylor-Convery
Composed at JTC Imagineering, Santa Maria, CA